MVFOL

D1123485

In-Line Skating

A Level Two Reader

By Cynthia Klingel and Robert B. Noyed

The Child's World®

2

In-line skating is a lot of fun.

It is a lot like ice skating.

In-line skates look like ice skates. Both sports have a boot for your foot. The boot comes up high over your ankle.

In-line skates have four wheels. Most skates have a brake on the back. The brake helps you slow down or stop.

There are many places to
in-line skate. Some people
skate indoors.

You should always wear a helmet. There are special pads for your knees, wrists, and elbows.

You can do many things on in-line skates. Good skaters can do tricks. Some people play hockey.

13

It is easy to fall when you are in-line skating. It is important to wear safety gear at all times.

Many people skate outside
on sidewalks or trails.
There are parks just for
in-line skating.

18

It is important to skate safely. You do not want to go too fast.

After some practice, it will

be easy to in-line skate.

Have fun and be safe.

Index

To Find Out More

Books

Savage, Jeff. *Top 10 In-Line Skaters.* Springfield, N.J.: Enslow Publishers, 1999.

Sullivan, George. *In-Line Skating: A Complete Guide for Beginners.* New York: Cobblehill Books, 1993.

Web Sites

International In-line Skating Association Resource Center
http://www.iisa.org/
Provides information for beginning and experienced skaters, as well as safety tips and a history of the sport.

Note to Parents and Educators

Welcome to The Wonders of Reading™! These books provide text at three different levels for beginning readers to practice and strengthen their reading skills. Additionally, the use of nonfiction text provides readers the valuable opportunity to *read to learn*, not just to learn to read.

These leveled readers allow children to choose books at their level of reading confidence and performance. Level One books offer beginning readers simple language, word choice, and sentence structure as well as a word list. Level Two books feature slightly more difficult vocabulary, longer sentences, and longer total text. In the back of each Level Two book are an index and a list of books and Web sites for finding out more information. Level Three books continue to extend word choice and length of text. In the back of each Level Three book are a glossary, an index, and a list of books and Web sites for further research.

State and national standards in reading and language arts emphasize using nonfiction at all levels of reading development. The Wonders of Reading™ fill the historical void in nonfiction material for the primary grade readers with the additional benefit of a leveled text.

About the Authors

Cindy Klingel has worked as a high school English teacher and an elementary teacher. She is currently the curriculum director for a Minnesota school district. Writing children's books is another way for her to continue her passion for sharing the written word with children. Cindy Klingel is a frequent visitor to the children's section of bookstores and enjoys spending time with her many friends, family, and two daughters.

Bob Noyed started his career as a newspaper reporter. Since then, he has worked in communications and public relations for more than fourteen years for a Minnesota school district. He enjoys writing books for children and finds that it brings a different feeling of challenge and accomplishment from other writing projects. He is an avid reader who also enjoys music, theater, traveling, and spending time with his wife, son, and daughter.

Readers should remember...
All sports carry a certain amount of risk. To reduce your risk while in-line skating,
skate at your own level, wear all safety equipment, and use care and common sense.
The publisher and author will take no responsibility or liability for injuries resulting
from the use of in-line skates.

Published by The Child's World®, Inc.
PO Box 326
Chanhassen, MN 55317-0326
800-599-READ
www.childsworld.com

With special thanks to the Motzko and Cleveland
families, and the Ramp, Rail, and Roll Indoor
Skate Park in Mundelein, IL, for providing the
modeling and location for this book.

Photo Credits
All photos © Flanagan Publishing Services/Romie Flanagan

Project Coordination: Editorial Directions, Inc.
Photo Research: Alice K. Flanagan

Library of Congress Cataloging-in-Publication Data
Klingel, Cynthia Fitterer.
In-line skating / by Cynthia Klingel and Robert B. Noyed.
p. cm.
"Wonder books."
Summary: Simple text describes in-line skating, discussing where
and how to do it, what the skates look like, and how to stay safe.
ISBN 1-56766-816-X (lib. bdg. : alk. paper)
1. In-line skating—Juvenile literature.   [1. In-line skating.]
I. Noyed, Robert B.   II. Title.

GV859.73 .K45   2000
796.21—dc21   99-057723